BABY'S FIRST BOOK

by Garth Williams

This is a work of fiction. Names, characters, places, and incidents either are the product of the author's imagination or are used fictitiously. Any resemblance to actual persons, living or dead, events, or locales is entirely coincidental.

Copyright © 1955, 1959, renewed 1983, 1987 by Random House, Inc.
All rights reserved. Published in the United States by Golden Books, an imprint of Random House Children's Books, a division of Random House, Inc., New York.
Originally published in 1955 by Western Publishing Company, Inc.
GOLDEN BOOKS, A GOLDEN BOOK, A LITTLE GOLDEN BOOK, the G colophon, and the distinctive gold spine are registered trademarks of Random House, Inc.
A Little Golden Book Classic is a trademark of Random House, Inc.
www.goldenbooks.com
www.randomhouse.com/kids
Educators and librarians, for a variety of teaching tools, visit us at
www.randomhouse.com/teachers
ISBN: 978-0-375-83916-0
Library of Congress Control Number: 2005934621
30 29 28 27 26 25 24 23
Printed in the United States of America First Random House Edition 2007

GOLDEN BOOK • NEW YORK

"Get up, sleepy-head!"
says Teddy Bear.

"Tick tock, get up!" says the clock.

I hang up my pajamas.
I help make my bed.

I take a bath.
I brush my teeth.
I brush my hair.

I put on my jeans.
I put on my shirt.
I put on my shoes and socks.

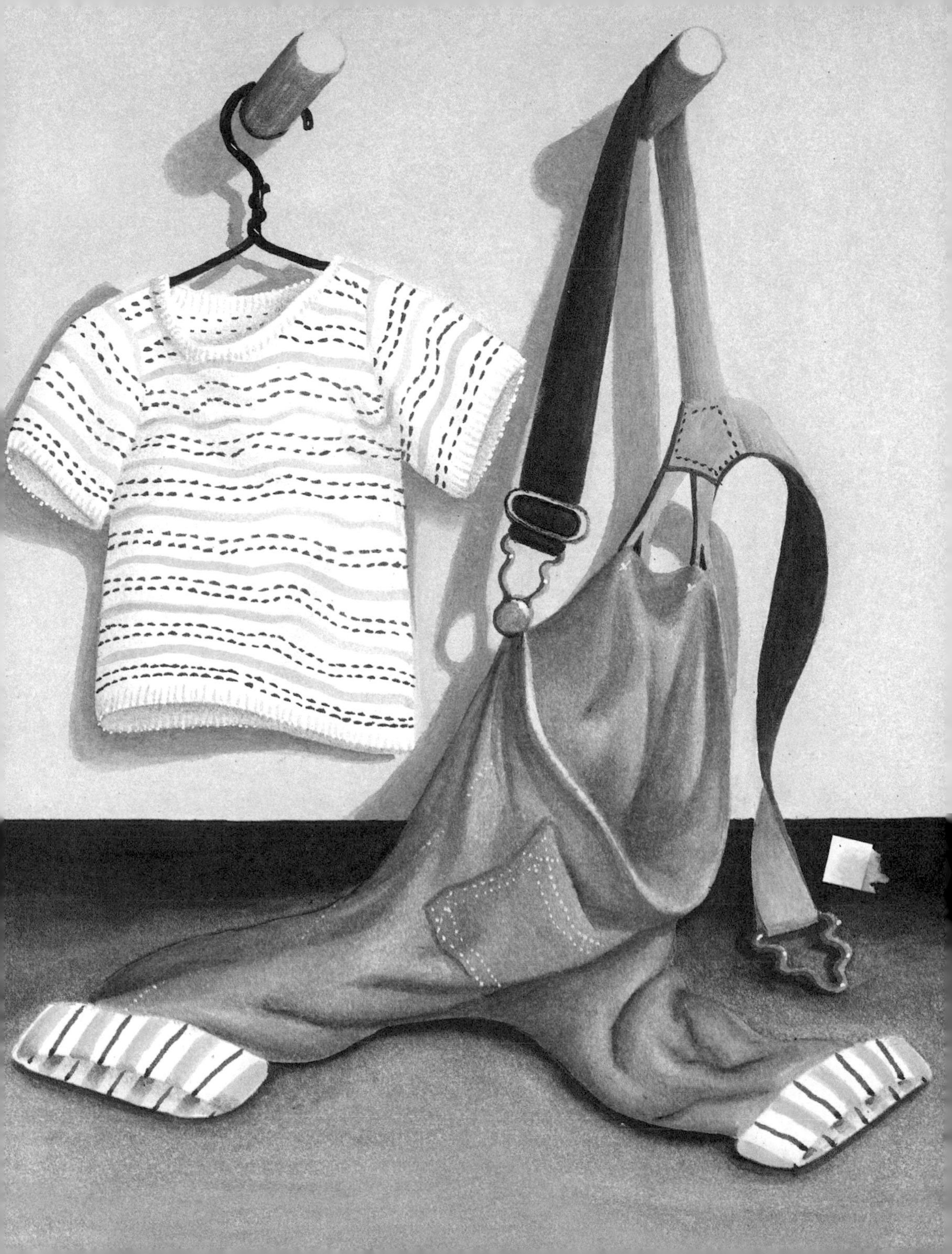

I sit on my chair.
I pick up my spoon.
I eat till my dish is empty.

My toys are waiting—
my car, my train,
my speedy jet plane.

US
41
2

Dolly is dressed up now.

She is looking in the mirror.

Baby Doll is awake.

And Kitten has finished his nap.

I play with my ball.

I play with my puppy.

I see three balloons—

and a bird singing in the tree.

I am hungry.
I eat some fruit.

But best of all, I like
my cake . . .

And my present,
a paintbox.